The Lost Flower Children

The Lost Flower Children

JANET TAYLOR LISLE

ILLUSTRATED BY SATOMI ICHIKAWA

SCHOLASTIC INC.

New York Toronto London Auckland Sydney
Mexico City New Delhi Hong Kong

Patricia Lee Gauch, editor

ISBN 0-439-17921-1

12 11 10 9 8 7 6 5 4 3 2 1   0 1 2 3 4 5/0

Printed in the U.S.A.   40

First Scholastic printing, April 2000

Book design by Gunta Alexander. The text is set in Bembo.

For Verena Middleton,
our Aunt Bee

One

It would never have been Olivia's idea to go live with Aunt Minty. If anyone had asked her, she would have said:

"That's the worst idea I ever heard of. Nellie will hate it. You can't send us there."

But their mother had died during the winter and no one seemed to want to ask her anything anymore. When Olivia tried to explain what a mistake it would be (for Aunt Minty was a very, very old lady!), Pop looked at her with tired eyes and said:

"The trouble is, Livy, I'm always on the road. And there's nobody here I can get to look after you. Just try it for the summer and see how it goes, and I'll call every chance I get, I promise."

So at the appointed hour of the appointed day, they set out on the two-hour drive to Aunt Minty's house with a great bundle of possessions. Nellie brought twenty-three stuffed animals—her entire brood—which she needed in order to get to sleep at night. She packed them into the back seat before anyone could stop her.

"Now this we cannot have," Pop said when he came out and saw what Nellie intended.

"She needs them," Olivia explained. "She absolutely does."

"Not all of them, no she doesn't. That is pure silliness," Pop said, while Nellie glared at him through angry tears. She spread her arms far out to prevent the animals from being taken back in, and her whole mouth began to tremble. Olivia couldn't bear it.

"Yes, she does need them!" she cried to Pop. "All of them! They are her family, you know. Nellie would never think of leaving *them* behind."

It came out so fiercely that Pop was shocked and turned away, and they all climbed into the car without another word.

Nellie gazed straight ahead over the back seat and didn't say thank you to Olivia or even glance at her as they drove away from the house. She didn't have to. With Mama gone, Olivia was the one who watched out for her now, and they both knew it.

The sisters had visited Aunt Minty before, though never to stay. Olivia remembered her house very well from when they used to come with Mama for lunch. She remembered Aunt Minty's garden. It lay off the side porch, a big horseshoe-shaped garden surrounded by hedges. A stone wall with a stone bench set into it was down at the end.

There must have been a time when the flower beds were elegant and well tended, but they weren't anymore. Aunt Minty had grown creaky and less interested in the fine arts of weeding and pruning, and so the flowers had crept together into dense, tangled clumps, and vines and wild grasses had pressed boldly in around them.

Stepping out of the car, Olivia caught a glimpse of this tangle and press through a hedge. It seemed to her that the garden was more neglected than ever, and she was certain that this was not the right place for them to stay. She was about to tell Pop that they must leave immediately and he should put their things right back in the car, when Aunt Minty appeared in a shabby straw hat.

She looked as small and fine-limbed as a bird and spoke in such a soft voice that Pop had to keep bending over and saying, "Excuse me? I didn't quite hear that."

Olivia caught his eye and scowled desperately, but he pretended to ignore her.

"Please *do* come into the garden," Aunt Minty said in a wrenlike chirp, so everyone went and Pop shouted out:

"Beautiful! Hasn't changed a bit. Did you girls know that your Great-aunt Minty was once a famous gardener? Stand over by that stone bench, I want to take your picture."

Nellie refused to move at first. She was still angry about the threats against her animals. Then she looked at Pop's face and saw how things were going to be, no matter what, and changed tacks.

"I'll do it if Livy does," she said. "Come on, Livy. Well, *come on!*" She was in the bossy fives that year and liked nothing better than to order people around.

"This is going to be a before-and-after picture," said Pop, squinting through the camera while he tried to focus the lens. "Here you are before, thin and wan and—"

"What is 'wan'?" Nellie asked.

"It means pale," Olivia said, without looking down. She had the sort of mind that took in words like a sponge.

"Well, I'm not!" Nellie said, deciding now to be insulted.

"You wait till you taste your Aunt Minty's hot apple pie and ice cream!" Pop bellowed from behind the camera. "Not to mention her blueberry muffins! You girls are going to be two happy stuffed chickens by the time I get back."

This was so much the opposite of anything anyone could expect that Olivia glanced over to see what Aunt Minty thought. She was standing off to one side pressing her hands together as if she were praying, which she most likely was because she hadn't wanted them any more than they had wanted her.

"The whole summer? Glory!" was what she had said on the telephone when she first heard Pop's idea. Olivia had listened in on the conversation; she was an expert phone bug and could lift up so nobody ever knew she was there.

"Oh no, Gerald. It's much too late for me to be taking on that kind of responsibility. How old did you say little Nellie is now?"

"She's five and a half, Olivia is nine, and no it isn't too late. And never will be," Pop declared in his best salesman's voice. "You took care of me one time when I was a sprout." (Minty was *his* aunt really.) "And anyhow, you've just got to take them, Mint. Honest to God, you're my last resort!"

Olivia looked over at Aunt Minty again. Her old straw gardening hat had holes in it. Wisps of yellowy-white hair straggled through, as if they were part of some overgrown plant too.

"Come on, smile!" Pop yelled. "Say Chunky Chopped Cheese."

"Chunky Chopped Cheese," Nellie and Olivia murmured together.

"Now don't let me forget when I come to pick you up at the end of September—"

"At the end of August," Aunt Minty said softly.

"I mean at the end of August, don't let me forget to take the 'after' picture. I want to see the big difference. I want to see how you grew three inches and learned to tango!"

Nellie began to snuffle at this because it was what Pop always said when he was about to leave on a long trip. But he swooped down and gave her and Olivia big bear hugs and was in the car backing out the driveway so fast that she didn't have time to start up a real roar. Then Aunt Minty, looking as shaken as both the girls, said in a doubtful voice, as if it might have galloped off in the meantime:

"I believe I saw a plate of chocolate chip cookies in the kitchen a while ago."

Olivia took Nellie's hand and marched her into the house, and that was that. They were there, stuck, dumped at Aunt Minty's in such a way that even Aunt Minty herself felt left behind.

Two

It was clear to Olivia from almost the first minute that Aunt Minty was in no way prepared to deal with Nellie. This was not her fault. It was Pop's fault for badgering her into having them and then for leaving them there without a word of warning, but that didn't change anything.

Nellie was little but she was very complicated, and it took a kind of genius to figure her out. If you couldn't figure her out, or didn't do it fast enough, she went into a raging howl that froze dogs in their tracks and drowned out the civilized world for miles around. (Pop had said this.)

Poor Aunt Minty knew nothing about this howl as, gentle as a gray dove, she led them into her old-fashioned kitchen. She did not know that there were certain ways of doing things that were right in Nellie's mind, and others that were wrong, and that you must never make a mistake and stumble into the wrong way.

For instance, Nellie must always put her socks and shoes on first in the morning, then step into her underwear, then her pants, then put on her shirt, because she believed, like the tide, in rising from the ground. This rule was engraved in gold in her mind. You did not want to suggest, however nicely, that there might be an easier way.

Another of Nellie's rules was that she must always walk upstairs facing down and walk downstairs facing up. It took extra time, but everyone had to wait. If you didn't want to wait, like Pop, the whole morning could be wasted while Nellie screamed like a red-eyed baboon and refused to go anywhere at all.

There were a hundred other golden rules like these that no one except Mama had ever known. Now that she was gone, they were impossible for any other person to learn completely, although Olivia was trying. At home, she had been teaching Pop, who often lost his patience and did not always see the importance of rules that came out of anyone but him. But at least he was Pop and knew what to expect.

A whispery old aunt is a very different matter. Olivia saw that she would have to be constantly on guard, ready to leap forward and steer Aunt Minty away from pitfalls that, once she fell into—who knew what she would do? Drop down dead? Run away? Lock Nellie in a closet and call the police?

Indeed, hardly two minutes had passed in Aunt Minty's kitchen that first day before pitfalls began to open like volcanic craters on all sides of her.

One of Nellie's rules was that she could not eat any food that had more than two identifiable things in it. When she was graciously offered a chocolate chip cookie by Aunt Minty, she naturally expected it to be the right kind. Unfortunately, lurking like evil beetles inside where no one could see were nuts as well as chips.

"No!" Nellie screamed, spitting out a big bite onto the floor. "I hate you!" she yelled down at the half-chewed lump, and kicked her foot so hard that her shoe shot off and landed on top of the refrigerator.

Aunt Minty looked very alarmed by this. Olivia thought for a moment she might even faint, but she recovered after a minute and offered Nellie a little dish of chocolate pudding that was going to be for supper.

"Would you mind having it now?" Aunt Minty asked, so sweetly that Nellie was pleased and agreed to eat it. Though she wanted her real pudding later of course, otherwise . . .

"Of course," Aunt Minty said quickly.

They ended up having a surprisingly pleasant talk about a strange smell that was in her kitchen—not like home at all. ("Old wood, I'm afraid," Aunt Minty said.) And about a cricket that appeared suddenly on the counter and hopped down the sink drain. Nellie was upset when it didn't come up again.

"Don't worry. Aunt Minty won't turn the water on till after supper," Olivia said.

"I won't?" said Aunt Minty, who had been about to rinse out their milk glasses.

"That will give him time to escape, one way or the other," Olivia said.

"Or give *her* time," Nellie said. "What if the cricket's a girl?"

"In that case, we could let her have till tomorrow morning," Aunt Minty offered generously, catching on at last. Olivia gave her an encouraging nod.

Aunt Minty then suggested that the sisters go upstairs to look at their room, and immediately broke another golden rule by trying to help Nellie down from her high kitchen stool. This was the sort of thing no one was permitted to do anymore, so they had to live through another earsplitting scream. Aunt Minty received a sharp push as well.

"Nellie hates help," Olivia explained. "She has to do everything herself, unless she tells you."

"I'm sorry. I didn't think," Aunt Minty said. Nellie didn't look so ready to accept her apology this time, and gazed at her with icy resentment. When they went upstairs, Nellie took an especially long time going up backwards.

"How did this rule get started?" Aunt Minty asked Olivia in a low voice, while they waited at the top for her to arrive.

"We don't know," Olivia murmured. "And don't ask Nellie or you'll break another rule."

"Which rule is that?" Aunt Minty whispered.

"The one that says no one can ask her why any rule is a rule."

By bedtime, Aunt Minty had broken so many rules and plunged into so many of Nellie's pitfalls that she began to look rather wan herself. Olivia told her she could go downstairs if she wanted and she would take over getting them both ready for bed.

"I know how. I've been doing it at home," she assured Aunt Minty, who went away immediately. This pleased Olivia. She had been afraid that Aunt Minty might try to interfere with the way they did things. They'd had some bad times with a number of very stupid sitters during the last few months.

The rest of the evening went quite well, although getting twenty-three stuffed animals and Nellie into the half-size child's bed that Aunt Minty had provided for her was impossible. Someone was always falling on the floor, which made Nellie shriek with frustration and despair. Finally Olivia gave her her own big bed, and took the little one for herself, though her legs were too long for it when she stretched them out.

Aunt Minty said nothing about this change when she came to say goodnight. Olivia saw her looking thoughtfully at Nellie, though.

"Wouldn't you like to stay up a bit later and come downstairs with me?" Aunt Minty asked Olivia as she was about to leave, since it did seem rather early for a nine-year-old to go to bed.

"Oh no, she can't!" Nellie exclaimed.

"Well, I could if I wanted," Olivia said carefully, "but I like to stay with Nellie. It's the way we've been doing it."

Aunt Minty nodded and said, "Goodnight, my dears," and turned out the lights.

When she had clumped away down the hall, Nellie fell asleep instantly. Olivia lay awake listening to her sister's deep-sleep breathing while her own eyes roved about sharp as flashlights in the dark. She examined their strange new room: the little couch with their clothes draped over the arms, the bright spray of light that came in through the partly closed door, the aqua-colored walls with their odd texture of hardened oatmeal.

The ceiling had a network of cracks running all over it, like boundary lines on a map of heaven. Only it was a map of heaven that no one had ever seen before, and needed someone to fill in if it was going to be real. After she had thought out the route she would take to the bathroom, in case Nellie had to go late at night in the dark, Olivia began giving names to some of the heavenly countries—Cloudlandia, Angelmark, Darkestonia. She was just starting to feel a little sleepy when Aunt Minty appeared at the door of their room and asked:

"Is someone crying in here? I thought I heard someone crying."

Olivia sat up. "No, you didn't."

"I thought maybe someone might be homesick," Aunt Minty said, coming forward and peering down at both their faces. Nellie's face looked especially peaceful, lying in the middle of all her animals in Olivia's bed.

"No, no one is," Olivia said scornfully. "That is pure silliness." Aunt Minty nodded and went quickly away down the hall.

But after she left, her question rushed into the place in Olivia's head where she kept her sadness. The face and feel of her mother came achingly out and tears began filling her eyes and running down her cheeks onto the pillow. For a while, she almost wished Aunt Minty would come back and ask her the question again. She was even thinking of calling out, when Nellie shouted something in her sleep that sounded like, "Give me my rattle!"

This was so ridiculous, and at the same time so bossy and maddeningly like Nellie, that a laugh rose like a big bubble inside Olivia's chest. Ha-ha-ha! Olivia burst out laughing right through her tears. At this, the sadness, which was also a kind of fright, sealed itself away in her again and she closed her eyes and went to sleep.

Three

The next week was a very hard one for poor Aunt Minty. There was so much for her to learn. It was not only that she didn't know any of Nellie's golden rules, and so was frequently being howled at or glared at or causing a flood of tears. It was also that she knew almost nothing about children in general.

"Or she has forgotten," Olivia confided to Nellie. "She did once take care of Pop. I heard her say so."

"Did she never have any children that were hers?" Nellie asked.

"She never got married. She is an old maid," Olivia said severely.

"I guess that's why she doesn't know about us,"

Nellie said, sounding sympathetic toward Aunt Minty for the first time.

"But you'd think she would have more common sense," Olivia declared, which was what their mother used to say about people she disapproved of.

Olivia did not feel so sympathetic toward Aunt Minty after some of the things she had done. For instance, she gave Nellie a sharp knife at dinner to cut her meat, which Nellie might easily have stabbed herself with if Olivia hadn't taken it away.

Aunt Minty kept asking Nellie what time it was and then, most laughable of all, believing what she said.

"Five-year-olds can't tell time," Olivia had to inform Aunt Minty at last—a terrible embarrassment to Nellie, who had begun to wonder if, after all, she could tell time since Aunt Minty seemed to think she was always right.

More dangerously, one afternoon Aunt Minty suggested that the sisters walk to a store that was at least a mile away down a busy street for Popsicles. There was a sidewalk, but still . . .

"We are too young to walk that far alone," Olivia told her. "Our father would not like it."

Aunt Minty looked at them in surprise. "But you seem so clever and reliable," she said.

"We are," Olivia said. "But things could happen. It's not as safe out there as it used to be. I mean, when you were young."

Aunt Minty agreed absolutely that this was so. Olivia was completely right, she said, and she, Aunt Minty, was a harebrained old fool to imagine such a thing—walking to the store! What would she think of next?

"You could think of driving us," said Nellie, who was fond of orange Popsicles.

"Well, so I could," Aunt Minty replied, and she immediately did. She was the sweetest person, and so constantly in a state of feeling sorry for her mistakes—whereas Pop and several sitters had been driven into unreasonable rages by theirs—that Olivia's hard view of her softened a bit.

"If only Aunt Minty would stop trying to get us friends," Olivia said, with a quick glance at Nellie one

day during the second week. "She is always trying."

"We don't want them," Nellie said. "My animals don't want them either."

"Of course not," Olivia said. She looked across the garden and heaved a tiny sigh.

They were often out in the garden. Aunt Minty liked to stump around with a basket and clippers, murmuring to the flowers and snipping here and there. You could not call it pruning since nothing ever was changed. The flower beds were too far out of control to be brought back to order by one little old woman, even if she had once been a famous gardener.

Olivia and Nellie had disliked the dense, leafy chaos of the place at first, and had chosen to stay up on the porch to do things: puzzles, drawings, Chinese checkers, reading Aunt Minty's old books, of which

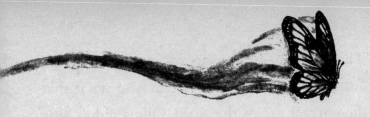

there were hundreds stacked in closets and on shelves throughout the house. But gradually, as the days went by, the girls began to come down.

They captured an orange and black monarch butterfly in an old butterfly net that Aunt Minty kept in the porch chest. And then released it because it looked so terrified.

They hunted for four-leaf clovers, but never saw one.

They found an abandoned wasp nest being lived in by a mouse in the stone wall at the garden's end. Peering inside, they could just see the whiskered tip of his nose turned bravely to face them, ready to fight if necessary.

Nellie began to bring some of her animals down onto the grass for daily outings.

"They have been indoors too much. They are wan," she said, looking over at Olivia to see if that was the correct use of the word. Olivia didn't hear her, though. She was staring dully out into space, as if her mind had gone off and left her body behind.

It was at these moments that Aunt Minty would bring up having friends over. She didn't mean real friends, she meant visitors. For instance, there were two children just down the road, a sister, ten, and a brother about Nellie's age, whom she was always trying to get them to meet. Their names were Jill and Leo. Their parents worked during the day and they were looked after by a real trained nanny who knew the very best ways of taking care of children. ("Poor things," Olivia whispered to Nellie.)

There was a local swimming pool where these children, and many others, went in the afternoon. A lifeguard was on duty to watch over everyone. "We could go if you want to," Aunt Minty offered.

"Nellie can't swim," Olivia said. "She doesn't like to go in water."

"*You* could go," Aunt Minty urged. "Wouldn't you like to? Just for a change?"

"She can't without me," Nellie said.

Olivia shook her head. "No, not without Nellie."

Well then: Someone Aunt Minty met in the library had a daughter a little older than Olivia, eleven or so, who was interested in collecting butterflies. "Arabella is her name. Don't you think that's nice? Shall we have her over for lunch?" Aunt Minty asked brightly during breakfast.

And again: Two boys rode their bicycles slowly past the house one morning, looking in curiously. "They want to see the garden," Aunt Minty said. "They've heard it was owned by a writer long ago and is the scene for some of his stories. Shall we have them in?"

The answer to all these questions was no. Olivia looked wistful sometimes, but Nellie was firm.

"There are too many of us already," she said, looking around at her animals, which she had arranged in conversational circles on the grass.

"Yes," Olivia would agree. "We're too busy right now."

"How about next week?" Aunt Minty pressed. "We could serve orange Popsicles."

This was so clearly a low trick aimed at undermining Nellie's opposition that the sisters did not even dignify it with an answer.

"She must think I am a little baby to try that stuff," Nellie complained later.

"All this friend business is beginning to get on my nerves," Olivia replied. "Do you think we should let her invite one person over, just one for one time only, so she'd stop bothering us?"

"We can't," Nellie said. "My animals would feel left out."

"Why? They could be with us in the garden just the way they are now."

"But no one would be paying attention to them because they'd be playing with the friend," Nellie said. "The one thing my animals can't stand is getting left out." She began to look very worried and upset, so Olivia went and sat down with her on the grass.

"Don't worry, I would never let Aunt Minty invite anyone over," she said. "She's just gotten to be such a pest. You're absolutely right about your animals. They would hate it."

"I know I *am* right," Nellie said in a quivering voice. Her eyes were suddenly full of tears. "We don't need anybody else, do we, Livy?" she asked, putting her arms around her sister. "Can't we just have each other and nobody else? That way, no one can get left out."

By now, Nellie's eyes had overflowed and tears were streaming down her cheeks. Olivia gave her the kind of bear hug Pop would at such moments.

"Don't worry, Nellie," she whispered. "We won't have anybody else."

Four

There were few hours in the day when Aunt Minty was not wearing her ratty old gardening hat. Nellie and Olivia became used to seeing her cooking dinner or washing dishes in it, sewing or reading newspapers in it, shopping at the food store and so on. Once, she even wore it to the dentist, who had to ask her to remove it before she got in the chair.

Olivia was embarrassed—what a stupid thing to do!—and moved to a seat across the waiting room, hoping people wouldn't see they were together. She thought of Mama, who was smart and pretty and understood how to act in public. She would never have worn such a hat.

Nellie was not embarrassed, though. She took the hat and held it carefully on her lap until Aunt Minty came out from her appointment and thanked her.

"Can't think straight without my hat," Aunt Minty declared, putting it back on and mashing it down idiotically to just above her eyes. Across the room, Olivia scowled with disapproval.

One morning, Aunt Minty appeared wearing her hat for breakfast. It was even more squashed and out of shape than usual, as if she'd put it on in a rush or perhaps even slept in it. The sisters wondered if something was wrong, but she served them a delicious breakfast of pancakes and sausages and, sensing the nearness of several large pitfalls, did not make the mistake of cutting up Nellie's pancakes or even asking her to use her fork to eat them.

Aunt Minty had something on her mind, that was obvious. Finally, as she was washing up the dishes, she turned to them and said in her soft, wavery voice:

"I was wondering if you girls might help me on a little expedition through the garden this morning? I want to find out where my lady slippers have gone to."

"Did somebody leave them outside?" Nellie asked.

"I think Aunt Minty means a flower," Olivia said.

"I do," said Aunt Minty. "I see your sister is someone who knows gardens," she remarked to Nellie.

"Livy knows everything," Nellie said. "She reads things in books and then she remembers. She can remember everything she ever read, and everything that ever happened to her, and she knows what people say even when they don't want her to because she listens in."

"No I don't," Olivia said, turning pink. She shot a warning look at Nellie.

"Yes you do!"

"That is silly," Olivia said, going over Nellie's head to catch Aunt Minty's eyes and persuade her of how silly it was.

"No it isn't, it's true!" Nellie shrieked, causing Aunt Minty's cheek to twitch. "Livy doesn't want people to know because they'll think she's spying."

"Hmm–mmm," Aunt Minty said, glancing at Olivia. She suggested they go outside right away, before the breakfast dishes were even finished, and get started on their slipper search. They all got off their stools and headed for the porch door. Olivia's heart was still pounding from how Nellie had revealed her secret. Luckily, Aunt Minty had not seemed to notice. She was concentrating on the lady slippers.

"They are quite small and easily missed," she said, as they came down the porch steps. "Their usual headquarters is down there near the stone bench. But slippers get around when you aren't watching."

"How do they do that?" asked Nellie, walking backwards down the steps in her usual way.

"Oh they do, that's all. That's the mystery of a garden. I certainly envy your good balance," Aunt Minty added to Nellie. "If I tried to do that I would break my neck."

"She has to do it," Olivia reminded her. "It's one of her golden rules."

Aunt Minty said her own golden rule was to walk forward, toes first, keeping a sharp eye out for people who were walking backwards so as not to collide with them.

In spite of herself, Olivia laughed. She had not known Aunt Minty could be so funny. But Nellie did not think it was a good joke at all, and when she saw them grinning at each other, she turned away hurt and went out into the garden.

"Well, well. I see the iris have bloomed in the night," Aunt Minty murmured, looking after her.

"Where?" asked Olivia.

She had to wait while Aunt Minty stopped to stuff her hair back inside her gardening hat. The wisps had more spring and energy in them than one would expect in an old lady's hair, and were always wanting to get out.

"There," Aunt Minty said at last, and pointed down the horseshoe-shaped lawn to an especially weedy bed where three enormous blue blossoms stood out on green stems nearly as tall as Nellie.

"Oh, they're beautiful!" Olivia couldn't help but exclaim. She felt amazed that anything so glowingly perfect could come out of this place. Aunt Minty nodded and raised her eyebrows mysteriously.

"It is magical, isn't it? I was passing by yesterday and heard them whispering among themselves. The flower children, you know. They said it was time."

Olivia smiled, and she was just going to raise her eyebrows mysteriously too, when she saw Nellie stop and look back in alarm. "Who are the flower children?" Nellie cried out.

"Oh, the spirits, I suppose you'd call them," Aunt Minty replied. "They live around this garden looking after things. Not the neatest of gardeners, are they? But they do keep things growing!"

"Don't worry, Nellie, they're only pretend," Olivia called, seeing how Nellie's face had suddenly tightened up. "It's make-believe, that's all. Aunt Minty heard it somewhere."

"It's an old, old story," Aunt Minty had to admit.

Nellie was immensely relieved to hear this. "Oh I knew it," she said. "I knew those children weren't real."

Olivia ran and caught up with her and put an arm around her shoulders. They walked down the garden together, leaving Aunt Minty to plod along behind. Olivia peeped back at her over an arm and thought: "Poor old Aunt Minty. Without me, she'd be lost."

The lady slippers were such slim, wispy things that it was almost impossible to see them without crawling around with your nose three inches from the dirt. Aunt Minty pointed out a picture in a book of what to look for. They really did resemble the sort of shoes fairy princesses might wear: soft and white with dark crimson tongues. Finally Olivia and Nellie found two, and were clearing away a thick patch of weeds that had all but choked them out, when Aunt Minty's voice came through the underbrush.

"Glory! Look at this!"

"What is it?" Nellie practically screamed. She'd become so excited searching for the lady slippers that she was ready to start seeing fairy princesses in every bush.

Aunt Minty's hat and head appeared through green leaves and she held up a little china cup. It was very dirty but, underneath the grime, showed a lovely bright blue. With its slender, looped handle and tulip shape, it looked as if it might have belonged in a child's playhouse.

Olivia took the fragile cup in her hand. "I can't believe it's not broken. How did it get in the garden?"

Aunt Minty shook her head. "That's what an old garden will do. Things drop down into it and get lost for years, and then all of a sudden they'll rise up out of nowhere into the light of day."

"How old do you think this cup is?" Olivia asked, handing it over to Nellie for inspection.

"Oh, there's no telling," Aunt Minty said. "I've been here seventy years, but the garden was here long before that. I've found pieces of plates, old forks and spoons, buttons, earrings, marbles, jackknives, everything you can imagine. One time there was a dog collar with the dog's name still on the tag."

"What name was it?" Nellie asked.

"Hmm." Aunt Minty creaked up off her old

knees and stood rubbing them thoughtfully. "Bound-less, I think. No, Bounder, that was it. I've still got it somewhere in the house."

"Did he get buried here?" Nellie said in a low voice.

"Might have. But he probably just lost his collar going through the underbrush, don't you think?"

"I think so," Nellie said gravely. At Aunt Minty's suggestion, she carried the little cup to the porch and carefully placed it on a step to save.

"Always keep what you find in an old garden," Aunt Minty told them. "It's got a purpose, most likely, for wanting to come back."

Soon afterward, the sisters grew tired and were ready to stop all garden expeditions, but Aunt Minty insisted on continuing the lady-slipper search "before they lose heart and decide to become extinct."

So for the remainder of the morning, Olivia and Nellie obligingly crawled here and there among the weeds and vines, which often towered over their heads or formed leafy tunnels around them. They found several much larger clumps of lady slippers, while Aunt Minty, whose knees finally gave out completely, pottered up and down the grass urging them on with her clippers.

Every once in a while, she would discover something else—"Glory, what have we here?"—and they would be introduced to tiny, fanlike lupine plants, just born out of the soil that morning and hardly an inch high. Or a pink and papery Oriental poppy thrusting powerfully up through a clump of crabgrass. Or a snail or one of the evil gray slugs, which Aunt Minty would fling over the hedge with a wild cry of "Invader, begone!"

"Aunt Minty has a good loud voice when she wants to," Nellie said to Olivia later.

"That is true," Olivia agreed. "She is not really a whispery person at all." But whether this was a good thing or a bad thing, she could not decide.

Five

Not long after Aunt Minty's discovery of the blue cup in the garden, Olivia made a discovery of her own, in the house. It was a book that came by the merest chance under her eye.

This, admittedly, was no usual eye. Nellie was right about Olivia's ability with books. She loved them with a passion and read faster than most grown-ups, somehow remembering every last detail. The trouble always had been to keep enough books around her so she didn't run out, though she was not against reading the same book three times in one day if that was all there was.

Aunt Minty's house had turned out to be a gold mine of books. There was no question of having to go to the library every week to drag home a new cartload for Olivia. The closets in Aunt Minty's house were packed with volumes, and the living room walls were covered with bookshelves, and all three bedrooms upstairs had bookcases loaded down and groaning. And this did not even count the attic, which was a dusty lunar landscape of piles and piles of books.

"Why do you have all these books?" Olivia asked her.

The answer was that she had inherited them. Her sisters and brothers and several cousins and an uncle and two very good friends among others had died and left them to her. It was a little sad to think of all these happy readers gone on to bookless worlds, but at least they had the comfort of knowing their books were in good hands.

"I know it's foolish, but I never could bring myself to give even one book away," Aunt Minty said.

"But you couldn't," Nellie exclaimed, "or you might have been haunted!"

Wherever it came from, Aunt Minty's vast inheritance was a great thing for Olivia, who never ran out of reading anymore, and she was tearing along through a bookcase in Aunt Minty's own bedroom one day when she came across a book, or rather a story in a book, that made her catch her breath. It was about a garden that reminded her, in a most unsettling way, of Aunt Minty's. And perhaps it even was her garden, because when Olivia showed her the book, Aunt Minty said:

"Oh yes. That's one of his."

"One of whose?" Olivia asked.

"It's one of the books the writer who used to live here wrote, years and years ago, when he was famous. Ellis Bellwether." Aunt Minty sighed. "We children all knew him and used to read his stories back then. Now his language is considered old-fashioned and nobody cares for him anymore."

Olivia took the book back to her room and read it again, front to back. The language *was* hard. The stories were rather dull. They were written in the style of fairy tales, about elves and magic brooks and spells that turned people to stone. But one story stood out from the others. It began: "There was once an old and beautiful garden shaped like a horseshoe . . ."

"Nellie, come listen to this."

"I can't now, Olivia. My animals are so tired. They need an afternoon nap."

"After you put them to sleep, come and listen. I'll be on the porch."

"Oh Livy, do I have to? I'm doing something else right now."

"Yes, you have to," said Olivia, in a voice that made Nellie look up in surprise.

The Lost Flower Children

There was once an old and beautiful garden shaped like a horseshoe with a stone wall at the end and a stone bench set into it. The flower beds were filled with flowers that flashed with color and attracted birds and wildlife of all kinds. It was a happy place to visit, always in use

for quiet meetings between friends or large birthday celebrations.

One night, unknown to anyone, a band of bitter, bad-tempered Green-Skin Fairies flew in by accident and took up residence in the tall hedges that grew along the garden's sides. They had lived hard lives, and been beaten down by the world (as invisible creatures often are), and they were appalled when they woke up in the morning to find themselves in a place so bright and pretty and clearly pleased with itself.

The blue irises, they noticed, were twice the normal size, which showed a shocking rudeness and disrespect of Nature. The June roses had the impudence to be pinker than a spring sunrise, and to last longer.

The violets, which were supposed to be shy and modest as young girls, had moved out of the hedge shadows and were swaggering around in the front border, while a clump of Lady's mantle that was meant to creep along the ground had risen up in a shameless froth of yellow-green blossoms.

"This is outrageous behavior," the lead Green-Skin said, and the other Green-Skins agreed. They did not like independence or high spirits of any kind, and were opposed to happy places in general because they so often encouraged these habits. And so they immediately set about to ruin the beautiful garden.

With green-eyed spite, they devised spells for shrinking blossoms and withering stems and root systems. They joined forces with several varieties of weed, and encouraged them to surround and strangle forward-moving plants. They attempted to smother the baby lupines with wet maple leaves and introduced dark gray slugs into the garden, which they bribed to eat all night, every night, until every new bud was devoured.

Any normal garden would have been devastated by this onslaught of evil, but the big, happy horseshoe-shaped garden went cheerfully on, overcoming all. The flowers banded together and fought off the slug attacks at night with specially concocted oils of their own. They defeated the withering and shrinking spells by growing in secret places not covered by the bad magic. They sucked all the water from the soil with their roots, and caused the weeds to dry up. The little lupines were rescued and guarded around the clock until they were big enough to fend for themselves.

The Green-Skins were infuriated by this pooling of imagination and inventiveness, and more furious that the garden succeeded in fighting off all their spells. They sat in the tall hedges fuming and plotting until their green wings turned a poisonous purple, but to no avail. The garden went happily on, growing just as it pleased and looking more beautiful every day.

But one day, the Green-Skins had their chance.

Late in July, a group of children came to the garden to have a party. What sort of party it was, the Green-Skins could not have said, for just as a curtain of shadow is drawn between the human world and the fairy world, making sprites nearly impossible for us to see, so the shadow curtain works equally upon fairy eyes, and human beings appear to them as shapes in a mist.

Still, peering through this mist, the Green-Skins understood that the event was a party. The children sat at a table set with pretty blue china, and they ate and drank and talked in a manner not unlike the Green-Skins themselves when they gathered for some merry occasion. (This was not often, of course, as Green-Skins rarely feel merry—perhaps once every five hundred years.)

Suddenly, the lead Green-Skin smiled and beckoned the others to his side. He'd had an idea, a very wicked idea that was made possible by a very evil spell he just happened to possess.

"Handed down from my rotten first cousin," the lead Green-Skin snickered. "He was too nice to use it, but we aren't. No, no, no!"

As the other Green-Skins watched, he drew from his back pocket, where it had been evilly kept for hundreds of years and sat upon and flattened to within an inch of its nasty life, a rare Transforming Spell.

"Oh! Ah!" The other Green-Skins backed away, because a Transforming Spell, as everyone knows, is the meanest, most unbreakable spell of all, and therefore seldom used.

"But will it work on a human?" one Green-Skin piped up. "Will it transform a human into something else?"

"It will," the lead Green-Skin said. "And not just one human, but many." He looked out at the garden full of children and snickered again.

"What is your plan, O Great Leader?" the Green-Skins chorused, and so the lead Green-Skin put his head low among his followers, and whispered to them what the evil plan would be.

Meanwhile, out in the garden, the party was in full swing. The children had risen from the table and were now playing games, running races, and having treasure hunts. But shortly they came back to their chairs to eat little cakes and iced cookies. They poured lemonade tea from a pretty blue teapot into the blue cups, and everything was so delicious that they soon finished it all.

One child, who was the smallest and most helpful, went back in the house to find more cakes. And this was how she became the only child to escape the Transforming

Spell that, in the next instant, the lead Green-Skin Fairy threw like a big greasy cloud over the whole party.

FLASH!—without warning, the spell was worked. One moment the garden rang with voices and burst with activity. The next, there was only the low rustling of wind blowing through leaf and blossom, for every child in the garden had been transformed into a flower.

Through the porch door, the smallest child saw it happen. Quickly she stepped back into the shadow, but too late. She was observed by the Green-Skin leader, and though he could not touch her with the Transforming Spell, he struck her dumb with another charm so that she would never tell a living soul.

For days afterward, the lost children were sought and begged for and called to come out of hiding. But the Transforming Spell was far too strong, and they remained rooted in the garden beds as roses, irises, lady slippers, lupines, delphiniums, day lilies, evening primroses, daisies, and tulips.

The Green-Skins were delighted to see how gloom and despair settled over the garden that had once been so happy. They were pleased to see the blue heads of the

irises droop and their leaves grow spindly, out of sadness for the lost children and those who called them. They cheered to see the new flower children acting so humble and dull-spirited, keeping company with slugs and low-life weeds, because they were under the Green-Skins' spell, of course, and forced to do so.

"Now this is a proper garden," the lead Green-Skin said with satisfaction. Then, because according to fairy law he was required to provide one countercharm by which the deadly Transforming Spell might someday have a chance of being lifted, he made up a particularly horrid one.

"Ha-ha!" he laughed. "No one will ever be able to work this!"

To doubly ensure it, and because the law required that he inform one person of the countercharm, he approached the one silent, left-behind child. She still came every day to see her old playmates, though she could not tell anyone why or what had happened.

"Ahem! Attention! I have in my possession a set of blue china cups and a teapot," the lead Green-Skin Fairy called to her, speaking from the safety of one of the tall garden hedges.

"It's too bulky and breakable to travel with, so I will leave it here, buried about the garden. You may look for this china if you wish, though one or two pieces will do you no good. If, by unlikely good luck, you should ever find all the cups and the teapot, and bring the set back together as it was on the table, the countercharm will break the spell. Your flower friends will be transformed into children again, and the party in the garden will continue as before—that is, before we so rudely interrupted, ha-ha!"

With this, the bad Green-Skin Fairies flew off to other places and other worlds and were never seen in those parts again.

The silent child set to work at once, spading up the earth. She dug all that day, but found nothing. The next morning she returned again, and the next morning, and the morning after that. For weeks she continued to dig in the horseshoe-shaped garden, then for months, but the blue china cups were hidden too well, nor did the blue teapot ever show its pretty spout.

The lost flower children remained under the Green-Skins' spell as roses and irises, lady slippers and lupines, delphiniums and day lilies, evening primroses, daisies, and tulips. They did not, however, continue to grovel and grow small as the Green-Skins had ordered. Quite the opposite and defying all the known laws of magic and spells, they grew to tremendous proportions and became ten times more beautiful and unusual than other flowers. For their beds were always groomed and weeded to perfection by the silent child, who, never giving up hope of seeing her friends again, came rain or shine to keep them company.

Daily she turned and raked the dirt, looking for the china. She removed the rocks, tossed out the slugs, cleared the vines, clipped the dead leaves. In this way, she came to know everything there was to know about growing things, and became famous as a gardener of great talent and wisdom, all without speaking a single word.

And so the Green-Skins were defeated once more, though not, as is so often the case, in a way anyone could have guessed. No garden in history was ever so well cared for and so loved as that of the lost flower children. And this despite the terrible Transforming Spell, whose evil was too powerful to undo—as some evils are in this world—and which remained unbroken. For never, even to the present day, has one piece of blue china ever been found.

♦ ♦ ♦

Nellie did not sit still for every bit of this rather long fairy tale. She jumped up and hung over Olivia's shoulder when there were pictures to be seen, and walked backwards up and down the porch steps during boring stretches, like when the flowers' names were listed. By the end, though, she was very quiet, and when Olivia looked up after the last sentence, she found Nellie staring at her with fixed eyes.

"We found a blue china cup," Nellie said.

Olivia nodded.

"Should we look for more? If there was one after

all this time, maybe there are more."

"We can't dig very well with just hands. We need shovels," Olivia said. "Aunt Minty has them in the garage."

"Well, let's go get them," Nellie said, starting to jump up and down.

Olivia paused. "Should we tell Aunt Minty?" she asked. But then another thought struck her and she seemed to know the answer. "Not yet, I guess. We'll just say we're going to weed the garden. "

"Okay!" yelled Nellie. "Come on, come on. *Come on!*" She raced down the steps for the garage, completely forgetting to go backwards.

"You know," said Olivia a little later, as they dug gently around the spot where Aunt Minty had found the first cup, "this flower children story is made up. It's fiction, like all fairy tales."

"Why does it have to be?" Nellie asked. "Why couldn't it be true?"

There was no good answer to this that would not hurt Nellie's feelings by going over her head, so Olivia merely shrugged.

She wasn't at all ready for what happened next. As she dug near the lumpy roots of the big, newly opened irises, her trowel touched something deep in the earth. At first, it seemed to be a stone. Two minutes later, when she had carefully dug the soil from around the object, she reached down with her fingers and brought up a second china cup. It was exactly like the other one, blue and tulip-shaped.

Nellie squealed with delight, and there was a look on her face that said she'd expected this all along. To her, the discovery wasn't extraordinary, just very exciting. But an odd shiver went through Olivia when she saw the cup. She sat back on her heels and looked around uneasily. A stillness she had not noticed before seemed to spread over the garden, and Aunt Minty's remark about the spirits who lived there came with new force into her mind.

They dug and dug for an hour more, but nothing else was to be found.

"I guess that's all they're going to give us today," Nellie said.

"Who?" Olivia asked.

"The lost flower children," Nellie whispered. "I think they're helping us."

"Why do you think that?"

"I don't know, I just feel it. Maybe their spell is wearing off and they're trying to come back."

"That's just a story," Olivia said firmly. "The writer, Ellis Bellwether, made it up."

"That's what *you* think!" Nellie exclaimed. "You just wait, you'll find out!"

They stowed their shovels back in the garage and agreed to dig again, secretly, tomorrow. But the next day it poured rain, and the day after was Sunday, when Aunt Minty had promised to take them to the zoo. If there were more blue china cups in the garden—and Nellie was absolutely sure there were—the lost flower children would have to be patient and wait a bit longer for them to be discovered.

Six

Twice a week, Pop called. After he had talked to Nellie, and then to Olivia, and sometimes to both at once if one or the other couldn't stand waiting, he would ask for a private chat with Aunt Minty.

"You girls get off now. We've got some business to discuss," he would say. They were supposed to hang up. Nellie always did, but Olivia, after she had put the phone down, would quietly pick it back up and listen in. It was the only way to find out what was really happening, because no one was going to tell her—she had learned that before.

When Mama was sick, Olivia would never have known half of what was going on without listening in on the phone. She'd also stayed awake at night to overhear the talk downstairs. If Mama's tests were bad at the hospital, or she had to have something done that scared her, Olivia would hear about it and be able to know it right along with her, though she never told her mother that she knew. The next morning after the bad news, she and Mama would both be pretending back and forth to each other.

Mama would be pretending that nothing in the world was wrong and she would be making jokes and keeping everybody on their toes, just as she always did. When they came home from school—play school in Nellie's case—even if Mama was back in bed, she never said where she'd been or what had happened. Olivia would pretend right along with her that everything was all right, partly for Nellie's sake, but also for Mama's. Because Mama wanted so badly for them to be happy, and untouched by anything that was going wrong, that Olivia decided to just let her go ahead and believe they were.

After all the listening in with Mama, there was no way Olivia could stop listening now. She had to keep on or she'd be lost, that was all. It wasn't spying, it was

. . . something else. So when Pop said, "Okay, you girls get off the line now," she'd put the phone down and then pick it right back up, soft and quick.

"How're things going, Mint?" Pop would ask, to start things off. You could tell by his voice he wanted to hear they were going all right, not the reverse.

Aunt Minty would say they were going all right.

Was Nellie behaving herself? Yes, fairly well. Was Olivia? Yes, Olivia was looking after Nellie like a little mother. They didn't want to have anybody over to play. Was that how they usually were?

Pop said they were close, no doubt about it.

Aunt Minty wanted to know if they'd had friends back home. Pop said he was sure they had, they were just getting used to a new place, feeling shy and so forth.

Well, I guess I won't worry about it, Aunt Minty said.

Is Nellie still walking upstairs backwards? Pop would always ask with a chuckle. Aunt Minty would assure him that she was.

Having listened in on a number of these phone

conversations, Olivia was pretty sure she knew what to expect from Aunt Minty. Aunt Minty was still tumbling into Nellie's pitfalls, but she was always sorry and always took Olivia's advice about how to avoid them the next time. In fact, after a month at Aunt Minty's, Olivia had the feeling that Aunt Minty was more or less under control. So she was completely taken by surprise when Aunt Minty announced at breakfast on the Monday morning following their day at the zoo, that she had invited Jill and Leo, the children down the street, over for lunch. In fact, they were coming in twenty minutes.

"Oh no. They can't," Olivia said quickly. Nellie shook her head, too.

"Well, they are already," Aunt Minty said.

"You didn't ask us," Olivia said. "You said you would ask us first."

"I don't remember saying that," Aunt Minty replied sweetly. "Did I say that?"

"Yes," Olivia said.

"I don't recall it at all. And besides, it won't hurt to have them. They are perfectly nice children.

I'm sure they are bored stiff over in their house with that nanny. Their friends have all gone to camp, I hear."

Nellie shook her head harder, looking first at Aunt Minty, then at Olivia, to whom she suddenly cried, "You promised you wouldn't let her!"

"Aunt Minty, this is not a good idea," Olivia began desperately. "I know it's not, especially not for Nellie. She won't like these children and they won't like her."

"How on earth does Nellie know she won't like them without even meeting them!" Aunt Minty retorted, in a loud, challenging voice that sounded very much like "Invaders begone!"

"She just does," Olivia pleaded.

"Yes, I do," Nellie echoed.

But Aunt Minty would not listen. She did not have the least notion about the vast, black pitfall that was cracking open under her feet. When, at nine A.M., a car pulled into the driveway with Jill and little five-year-old Leo inside, she went out to greet them as gaily and innocently as a little child herself.

Seven

If only there had been more time, Olivia might have thought of some way to fix things. She might have talked to Nellie as Mama used to, slowly and carefully, looking into her eyes and trying to see what she was most afraid of.

"I will be right beside you," Mama would have said. "Don't worry, Nellie, everything will be all right."

But Olivia had no time. Aunt Minty had not wished her to have any; she wanted nothing to interfere with her own plan. She assumed that once the guests were there, Olivia and Nellie would be polite hostesses. They would smile and act nicely, however they felt inside, because that was how girls were supposed to act, wasn't it? An old aunt like Aunt Minty would certainly think so. She wouldn't know, as Olivia absolutely did, that there are times when acting nicely can be too much to ask.

Looking through the half-open front door, the sisters watched the visitors being welcomed. Silently, side by side, they watched Aunt Minty shake hands with the nanny and beam friendly smiles down upon the faces of the children. They watched her invite everyone into the house. Olivia gave Nellie one last squeeze on her hand as the guests came near; then the visit began and they were being introduced.

Jill was a tall person with a long ponytail down her back and a sniffle. She said, "Hi—*sniff*—is this your house, *sniff*? I never knew anyone lived here . . . Oh, you're visiting your aunt, I see, *sniff, sniff.*"

The nanny handed her a tissue and said, "I hope you don't mind, Leo brought his trucks." They all looked down at Leo, who was small and square and carrying two large yellow trucks, one under each arm.

"This one's a dump truck and this one's a front-loader," he explained. "I've got two more in the car."

"Well, these are probably enough for now," said the nanny, who was younger than expected. She looked to Olivia like one of those college students that used to take care of them when Mama was in the hospital. They never would know where anything was.

"Oh no, he can bring them all in," Aunt Minty said. "We don't mind a few trucks, do we, girls?"

Olivia and Jill gazed at each other uneasily in the hall. The obvious question was how soon they could get away and start a real conversation, instead of all this fake, grown-up stuff. At least, Jill thought this. Olivia knew she was thinking it, and Nellie, standing nearby with a cold, blank face, knew it too. She stood completely still, watching Olivia with intense concentration.

"Come on, Nellie. Let's show them the garden," Olivia said in a polite hostess voice. She tried to take Nellie's hand, but it was knotted up into a hard fist that refused to come open.

"Thank you, Olivia, that's a fine idea," Aunt Minty said, and everyone trooped self-consciously through the house and out to the porch.

"Would you like to carry one of my trucks?" Leo asked Nellie on the way.

"No, thank you," Nellie said, keeping her eyes on the older girls in front of her. Jill had just said something to Olivia, who had nodded back.

"You can play with my trucks if you're careful," Leo went on, drowning out yet another remark that Jill made to Olivia, and which caused Olivia to smile. Nellie made no answer. She leaned forward to listen in on what Olivia was saying back to Jill. Something about swimming, or going to a pool.

"I've got a cement mixer and an earth mover in the car," Leo went on. "And at home I've got a Caterpillar tractor and a flatbed and a tow truck and a—"

"Will you please shut up!" Nellie screamed at him. She shoved him away and ran to catch up with Jill and Olivia.

Everyone swung around in surprise. Leo, who

had lost his balance and fallen over, began to sob like a baby.

Aunt Minty was shocked and caught Nellie by the wrist. "What is this? What is this?" she cried.

"He wouldn't stop talking and I couldn't hear," Nellie said, appealing to Olivia. "You and Jill were talking about swimming but I couldn't hear what you said."

"Oh Nellie, it was nothing! I was just saying—"

"Yes, it was something!" Nellie said, getting very hot and worried. She knew all the signs of being left out, and Olivia knew she knew. She came back quickly and took Nellie aside, away from Aunt Minty's hard grip, for a little talk. A minute later, the surface was calm again as the group toured the garden. But immediately new waves began to mount up.

Nellie followed close behind the older girls wherever they went: the backyard, the kitchen, the front steps, their bedroom. She tried to enter into their conversation, but she couldn't always understand what they were talking about and got things mixed up. This made her appear stupid and babyish, which was completely unfair. To get back, she began to cry out in a sneering voice, "Why is *that* so great?" whenever Jill said anything.

"Does she have to be with us—*sniff*—the whole day?" Jill was asking Olivia by the time they had come back to the stone bench at the garden's end. Olivia had promised to show her the wasp nest with the mouse inside.

"Yes, she does," Olivia said, glancing helplessly at Nellie. She never would have admitted it, but Nellie had started to wear on her nerves as well.

"Yes, I do!" Nellie shouted at Jill. "I'm not getting stuck with your dumb little brother."

"He's not dumb," Jill replied. "He's exactly your age."

"Age has nothing to do with dumbness!" Nellie announced. "You're as dumb as he is and you are nine."

"What is the—*sniff*—matter with her?" Jill asked Olivia in a superior tone that was meant to set up a special understanding between them. "Anyway, I'm ten, not nine. Your sister's the one who's dumb."

"I am not!" Nellie screamed. "You are! You are!"

"What a maniac," Jill sniffed to Olivia. "She belongs in the loony bin. How can you stand it? After this, why don't you come to my house, it's a lot more fun."

There was absolutely nothing Olivia could say to stop the dangerous drift of this conversation. She could not agree with Jill because Nellie was listening, and she could not disagree because it would have seemed impolite, and besides, she did want very much to visit Jill's house. She was sick to death of hanging around this boring, old garden, sick of watching out for Nellie and being so nice all the time. And, she was just turning around to tell Nellie to go away somewhere else if she couldn't act better when something hit her hard in the shoulder.

"Ouch!"

It was a stone.

"Ow!" cried Jill. She'd been hit too.

"Nellie, stop that!" Aunt Minty's voice was suddenly booming down the garden from the porch. But Nellie had somehow picked up a whole pocketful of big stones, and now she was hurling them, one after the other at Olivia and Jill.

"I hate you!" Nellie shrieked. "I hate you both!"

"Nellie, please!" Olivia cried out. It was too late for reasoning, though. Nellie was far beyond the place where she could stop, even if she had wanted to. Something wild had risen up inside her. It had taken over her body and mind and, as if she were a wounded animal fighting for its life, she threw and threw and threw the hard stones with fury and desperation blazing out of her eyes.

"Nellie, you're hurting us!" Olivia screamed, trying to stumble toward her. Jill had scrambled behind the stone wall.

Another step or two and Olivia might have reached Nellie, and pinned her arms in a big bear hug, and made her stop—but in the next moment a huge stone came flying through the air directly at Olivia's head. A terrific explosion rocked her back on her feet, and she felt herself fall off a cliff into darkness.

♦　♦　♦

The next thing Olivia knew, she was on the couch in Aunt Minty's living room and her head ached as if it had been split in two. Jill and Leo were standing near her feet, and the nanny was holding a cold cloth on her forehead.

"There you are," said the nanny. "Lie still and you'll be all right."

"You have a big red lump," Leo informed her. Jill stared at her and didn't say anything. Olivia knew she was thinking that this would never have happened if they had been at her house.

Aunt Minty stood over her then, and asked how she felt, and reported that Nellie had run off and was hiding somewhere in the garden.

"I'll go find her," Olivia said, sitting up at once, but everyone jumped forward and made her lie back. She did feel a little dizzy. "I'll go in just a minute," she whispered.

"Nellie will appear when she appears," Aunt

Minty declared in a high, shaky voice. "You stay right where you are."

In a little while, Jill and Leo had to leave. Lunch was out of the question after everything that had happened. Olivia had some chicken noodle soup and dozed for a while. When she woke up, it was late in the afternoon and she felt much better. But Nellie still wasn't back.

"I've called and called," Aunt Minty said. "Perhaps, if you feel up to it, you could try instead of me? I'm afraid she will never want to speak to me again. What a fool I've been!"

She looked very old and tired as she said this, and Olivia saw that her hands were trembling.

"Nellie!" Olivia called, out in the garden. "They've gone. You can come out now. I'm all right."

She walked slowly up and down the long flower beds, trying to see in between the leaves and weeds. The tangles were too dense and the shadows too dark to penetrate more than a foot or two. She felt a little as if she were calling to the lost flower children in the story, because the garden was so silent and unresponsive.

"Your animals are all alone!" Olivia cried. "They miss you and need you to come home!"

There was still no answer, which was unusual. Nellie always stood by her animals. Olivia began to feel a real panic rise up in her chest.

"Nellie!" she shrieked. "I'm scared! Where are you?"

A tiny rustle erupted in the bushes near the stone bench. A second later, Nellie stepped out. Her hair was wild and full of leaves, and her knees were dark with dirt.

She stood looking accusingly at Olivia for a moment. Then she rushed for her and flung herself around her like a drowning person grasping a log at sea. She buried her head in Olivia's chest and hung on to her for dear life. It seemed like an hour later, but was probably only a few minutes, when Olivia was finally able to say, huskily:

"I thought you were a lost flower child, gone forever."

"I think I was one," Nellie answered, still holding on. "For a little while I think that's what I was."

Gazing out the window, Aunt Minty saw them there at the end of the garden. By this time, they were sitting close together on the grass and talking quietly back and forth.

Aunt Minty drew her breath in raggedly, and let it out with relief. In a moment, she would walk down to them and say what a terrible mistake she had made, how she had not listened to Olivia and had misunderstood Nellie, and interfered in a place where she had no right to.

"Old fool," she muttered. "Have you forgotten everything you ever knew? They might have lost each other right then and there. But . . . what are they doing now?" she murmured, stepping closer to the window and peering out.

Olivia and Nellie had gone over to a flower bed and begun to dig in it with their hands. After a minute, Nellie ran off and came back with two trowels, and they went to work again, moving deeper into the garden.

Eight

Nellie found the third cup.

It lay about three inches down in the soil, near a plot of Shasta daisies that were blooming thickly despite being choked with grass.

"Exactly the same," Nellie said triumphantly, holding it up. She rubbed off some of the dirt so that the bright blue of the china shone out.

This was two days after Jill and Leo's disastrous visit, and though Olivia had mostly recovered from Nellie's stone, a big piece of gauze was still taped over the bruise on her forehead. Aunt Minty had apologized, "as she should have!" Olivia said. "From now on she'll ask before she invites anyone." Pop had called, everyone had forgiven everyone, and life at

Aunt Minty's was going on more or less as it had been. Except:

"Where are these coming from!" Olivia exclaimed, taking the mysterious tulip-shaped cup from Nellie and examining it closely. "There is no reason I can think of why these cups should be here, turning up after all this time. Do you think Ellis Bellwether buried them himself?"

"No, he couldn't," Nellie said.

"How do you know?"

"Because of the story, Livy. It was the Green-Skins who did it, to stop the children from being found. Now we're the ones who have to help them. We need all the cups for the countercharm to work."

"How many is all of them?" Olivia asked, feeling more confused than ever.

"Eight," Nellie said briskly. "A picture shows it in the book. And the teapot too, we can't forget that."

Nellie was a changed person. Whether it was the shock of hitting Olivia with the stone, or Aunt Minty's apology, or her long, solitary afternoon hiding in the garden, there was no knowing. Nellie was changed into a less babyish child who was not so interested in golden rules anymore. Instead, she wanted to dig, all day if necessary, in Aunt Minty's flower beds.

"My goodness," said Aunt Minty. "You are certainly getting at those weeds!"

She was transformed into a person who had to have "The Lost Flower Children" by Ellis Bellwether read to her every night at bedtime. And had to pore over the illustrations by herself every morning before breakfast.

"Did you notice how the Silent Child is 'the smallest and most helpful'?" Nellie asked Aunt Minty.

"Is she?" Aunt Minty said. "No, I hadn't noticed."

"Did you see how the Silent Child was struck dumb by the Green–Skins?" Nellie observed to Olivia. "That means she couldn't tell anyone anything when she was left behind."

"I know," Olivia said, watching in amazement as Nellie walked forward upstairs for the first time in months.

"But she could do something," Nellie said. "She could find the whole tea set."

"But she didn't," Olivia pointed out.

"But she will!" Nellie announced.

And three days later she found the fourth cup buried under a spindly clump of sky-blue delphiniums that had no right being alive at all after having been ignored for so many years, according to Aunt Minty.

She found the fifth cup in the lupines, which had grown up into lovely purple, many-blossomed flowers.

A week went by before the sixth cup turned up under a rangy patch of bright yellow evening primrose.

"I think the lead Green-Skin buried a cup under each flower child," Nellie said, holding up the sixth cup, victoriously. "That is how to find the rest of them."

"How?" panted Olivia, who was doing quite a lot of digging herself under Nellie's bossy direction. One thing that hadn't changed in Nellie was her bossiness.

"We should look around the flowers that are in the book. So far, we've found cups under the lady slippers, the iris, the daisies, the delphiniums, the lupines, and the evening primroses. Next let's try the roses."

"I am too tired," Olivia protested. "This work is too hard."

"Not for me," Nellie sang out, and she went off to ask Aunt Minty to point out a group of roses, so she could begin on them.

By now, Aunt Minty had been told about the other china cup discoveries, and had examined the cups herself. She was as mystified as Olivia as to how they had come to be there.

"Can I look at the story?" she'd asked Nellie, who kept the book in her bed along with her animals. "It's been years since I read it."

Nellie had brought it, and: "Remarkable," Aunt Minty had exclaimed when she finished. "I'd forgotten the garden was so exactly described. It is wonderful, isn't it, to see how many of the original flowers are still there—fighting off slugs and weeds but still alive underneath."

"Of course they're there," Nellie said. "Those are the flower children."

Olivia's eyes met Aunt Minty's over the top of Nellie's head, but neither one dared say a word against her. How could they when the astonishing cups, perfect copies of the tulip-shaped ones in the story's illustrations, kept appearing out of the dirt every few days?

The roses, lovely, old-fashioned pink ones, were barricaded by underbrush in a far corner against the

stone wall. Olivia and Nellie would never have guessed they were there, but Aunt Minty knew her garden as well as the inside of her own house, and pointed them out.

"They used to be climbers," she sighed, "when they were able to get up. In the old days, they grew all over this stone wall."

"Oh dear," said Nellie. "How will we know where to dig? I guess we'll have to go along the whole wall."

Olivia was exhausted even by the thought of this, and retreated to the porch to read. Nothing anyone said would get her moving again, so Nellie took on the job by herself.

Unfortunately, it was way beyond her strength, and by lunchtime she had made almost no progress. After lunch, she sat on the porch steps and gazed dejectedly down at the garden.

A sound of voices and bicycle wheels rose from the road. The boys who had so often come past before were pedaling slowly by again, looking curiously in the driveway as they always did.

In a split second, Nellie was on her feet and had disappeared. A minute later, Olivia looked up from her book to see her sister escorting two boys into the garden. They must have been ten or eleven at least.

". . . and so we've been digging for the rest," Nellie was telling them in a businesslike tone. "But it's a lot of work. That is Olivia," she added.

"Hi!" said Olivia, leaping out of her chair and blushing to be caught so off guard. She went forward eagerly.

The boys looked vaguely relieved to see her and said hi back. They asked if it was true about a lot of old cups being buried underground, and when Olivia said it was, they stalked around the garden with obvious interest. They had heard about Ellis Bellwether and how he used to live there. They hadn't read anything by him, though. Had any books been made into movies?

Olivia said no, she didn't think they had.

Nellie asked if they would like to help dig for more cups. They said okay, and sometime later, when Aunt Minty glanced outside, she was astounded to see two unknown visitors in her garden. They had been given shovels and clippers and, along with Olivia and Nellie, were down by the stone wall digging and clearing brush and talking like old friends.

"Glory!" exclaimed Aunt Minty, giving a twitch to her hat. She went right back in the kitchen to squeeze a batch of lemons for lemonade.

Nine

Nothing at all was found along the wall that afternoon, or the next morning when Jack and Morry—those were the boys—dropped by to try again. They rode off in disgust at noon. When they did not return the next day, or the next, Olivia's spirits sank and she withdrew again to the porch. Not even when Nellie found the seventh cup, in a place near the wall that they must have missed, did Olivia show interest.

"Don't you care, Livy?"

"Of course I do. I'm just so tired."

Partly, it was lack of sleep. She was reading not only during the days but also late, late into the nights, while across the room Nellie breathed her deep-sleep breaths and muttered from her dreams. Whenever

Nellie called for the bathroom, Olivia got up at once to take her down the dim hall, just as Mama used to do. If Nellie woke suddenly, scared in the dark, she had only to cry out "Livy!" And Olivia would answer, "I'm right here, Nellie. You can go back to sleep."

Sometimes when Nellie called, Olivia wasn't even reading, but just lying on her bed and staring up at the map of heaven over her head.

"What are you looking at?" Nellie asked her one night. She came over sleepily, and crept in beside her sister on the little bed, and looked up with her. Olivia explained about the map, and how she'd named all the countries of heaven, and some rivers and mountains and oceans as well.

"Every time I look up, I see something new, and then I name it," she said.

"Is Mama up there too?" Nellie wanted to know.

"She's just settling in," Olivia assured her. "She's like us with this map. She's figuring out the names of places and how to go around without getting lost. Every time she looks, there's some new place she hadn't noticed before, but pretty soon she'll know it. Then she'll feel safe."

"Does she miss us?" Nellie asked in a low voice.

"Yes she does," Olivia said. "And she always will."

"I miss her too," Nellie whispered, and she put her arms around Olivia and hugged her for a long while.

Afterward, she padded back across the room to her own bed and went to sleep. But Olivia lay awake thinking of their conversation. She did not always say exactly what she believed to Nellie, and now she wondered, as she often had before, if it ever could be true that Mama was somewhere thinking of them. Not up in the sky necessarily, but around and about, hovering invisibly, like Aunt Minty's flower children spirits.

Usually half of her said yes, it was possible, and the other half said no, I'm not sure. That night, suddenly, all of her wished with all her heart that Mama was there, and with the wish came a terrible, new longing to see her again. For a few minutes, Olivia didn't know how she could go on alone because "Nellie has me, but I have no one," she whispered.

When she said this, a cold wind seemed to enter

the bedroom. The place in her head where she kept her sadness suddenly blew wide open and she lay staring up with a trembling mind.

Then the map of heaven came into focus. Slowly and carefully Olivia went over all the names—the countries and rivers, the mountains and oceans—

until her breathing was steadier and her heart stopped pounding. The cold wind died away. The sadness went back into its secret place and sealed itself over. Nellie stirred and murmured in her bed, and little by little, Olivia's eyes closed too, and she let herself slide down a soft slope to sleep.

⬩ ⬩ ⬩

August arrived, and it was hard to keep digging for cups because every day a stifling heat settled over the garden. With afternoon came thundershowers and, in the distance, the eerie flicker of heat lightning. Mostly it was better to stay indoors.

"Olivia? Is that you?" Aunt Minty would ask, blinking into some dim recess where Olivia crouched, reading by a window, or hunched over on a stair.

"Yes, it's me."

"What on earth are you doing?"

"Nothing," Olivia would tell her. "Just trying to keep cool."

Nellie, on the other hand, grew more and more restless. If she could not dig, she would practice standing on her head. She would shinny up the front stair banister, tightrope-walk the kitchen counters, climb the bookshelves in the hall.

"Nellie! Get down at once!" Aunt Minty was always crying. "You are not a circus performer! Can't you do something else?"

She gave a lunch party for her animals on the

porch, but flew into a rage when Aunt Minty brought out the wrong kind of cookies on a plate. In the next moment, though, Nellie felt sorry for her outburst, and apologized.

"I don't think it was very fair of me when you were just trying to be helpful," Nellie said. "It isn't your fault if you're too old to tell good cookies from bad ones."

Aunt Minty was so undone by this compliment that she immediately dropped the whole plate of cookies on the floor.

Finally, though Nellie was the one who could not stop thinking about it, Olivia unearthed the eighth cup, late one afternoon.

It was in the dirt under a lavender plant, and she was not actually looking for cups at all but was leaning down with the clippers to snip a few sweet-smelling lavender sprigs. Aunt Minty had asked for them, to fill the little glass vase she kept by her bed. She would propose these sorts of errands when she thought Olivia needed "some stirring up," as she put it.

Olivia saw a flash of blue in the dirt and a minute later, with Nellie looking on, she pulled the cup from the thick, brown soil.

"Lavender is not one of the flower children flowers in the book," Olivia said, polishing the china on her shirt. "I guess there's no special way these cups are buried after all."

"Well, it doesn't matter because now we have eight!" Nellie cried. She was wild with joy. "All that's left is the teapot!"

She fell to her knees and began to dig frantically around the lavender again. She found nothing else, though, and soon the sweltering sun drove them inside.

Aunt Minty shook her head in wonder when she saw the last cup. When she heard it had been found near the lavender, she said: "Oh, that used to be a bed of day lilies, but I didn't like the color and dug them up years ago."

"How could you!" Nellie gasped. "You killed a flower child, you know."

"Glory!" said Aunt Minty. "I had no idea! But wait. Now that I think of it, those lilies didn't die. They kept on growing in the place where I tossed them. You can see them out the window, down by the field wall."

Nellie ran to look and saw that the field wall was awash with yellow and orange day lilies all along its length, and she was very relieved. "Maybe they liked the field better than the garden, anyway," Olivia heard her murmur to herself.

Aunt Minty seemed so honestly excited by the discovery of the eighth cup that Olivia felt a trickle of new interest too. It increased when they brought out all the cups and set them on the kitchen table, where they sparkled together like long-lost friends. Nellie had never been so ecstatic.

"Aunt Minty, sit down right now and start think-ing!" she said.

"About what?" Aunt Minty asked, sitting down as ordered.

"About where the teapot could be!" shrieked Nellie. "If we just had the teapot, the countercharm would work."

"Well, how should I know where it is?"

"Because it's your garden. You know every bit of it."

"That doesn't make any difference," Olivia said. But Nellie kept gazing expectantly at the old woman, and before long she was forced to rise to the occasion.

"Well . . . hmmm. Perhaps if I had another look at that book by Ellis Bellwether . . ." Aunt Minty said at last.

So Nellie brought the book downstairs again, and Aunt Minty opened to the story of *The Lost Flower Children*. There was nothing new there. She began to examine the pictures. They were beautifully drawn and surrounded by pretty borders, rather like flower beds themselves, filled with examples of different kinds of flowers. Woven among the flowers were little drawings of typical garden items: rakes and trowels, birds and butterflies, watering cans and wheelbarrows, flowerpots and . . .

"Aha!" cried Aunt Minty, in a voice that made Nellie jump.

"What is it?"

"Here is a rosebush with a cup drawn into it!"

"A cup! Why?"

"And here's a delphinium and another cup."

"That is impossible," Olivia said, feeling very queer suddenly.

Aunt Minty pushed the book toward her. "It looks to me as if the directions to the cups were in the borders of the pictures all along," she said. "If only we had known, you could have saved yourselves a lot of trouble. Here's another cup drawn with some lady slippers. Now what we have to find is—"

"A blue teapot!" Nellie shrieked. They all bent at once over the book.

It was there in one of the borders, of course. Not easy to see, because all around and over it were masses of red tulips, which gave the teapot a purple sheen and made it seem to be a shadow. "Very sly, this fellow Bellwether is," Aunt Minty declared.

"Red tulips! Have we seen any red tulips in the garden?" Nellie asked Olivia.

"No, I don't think so. I can't remember one."

Nellie's face fell.

Aunt Minty, however, tapped her finger and smiled. "You haven't seen any tulips because there aren't any now. But there were, in the spring before you came. They bloomed and went by."

"Show us where," whispered Nellie, with fiery eyes. She had just remembered how the cups themselves were shaped like tulips, which might very well be another clue.

So Aunt Minty took them out into the heat of the day, and showed them the place where the bright red tulips appeared every spring. It was now thick with wilted leaves and crabgrass, and also muddy from a recent rain shower. Never in their wildest dreams would Olivia and Nellie have thought of digging there. But the moment they set to work, they felt something pulling, pushing, nudging them on. Nellie believed it was the impatient flower children sending help again, and who could say this wasn't true, because not long after, her fingers ran into something. Digging down just below the surface of the softened earth, she uncovered the long, forked spout of an old-fashioned teapot.

Ten

From the moment Nellie lifted the vivid blue teapot out of the garden, Olivia began to look more closely at Aunt Minty. Eight old cups buried in a garden is unusual, but not beyond the realm of possibility. However the cups got there, they just might have gone unnoticed in a garden this size, and lain undisturbed in the earth over the years.

But a large, shining blue teapot lying on its side two inches down and with the lid still on? That, Olivia knew, would never have been overlooked. She gazed with deep suspicion at Aunt Minty, and was certain that she was interfering with Nellie again, despite what she had promised.

There was nothing to be done about it right

away, though, because Nellie was so excited. She wanted to put a table in the garden, with a lace table-cloth on it, just like the illustration in Ellis Bellwether's book.

She wanted to set the table with the blue cups, and napkins and plates of cakes and a big vase of summer flowers in the middle—the way the book showed.

"We have to do it just like the picture," Nellie ordered. "The Green-Skin leader said so. Otherwise the countercharm won't work."

To Olivia's surprise, Aunt Minty agreed.

"I think you are absolutely right," she said. "Everything must look the same—as much as possible, of course. I'm afraid I don't have a vase exactly like the one here." She tapped the book and looked worriedly at Nellie.

"Oh that's all right!" Nellie said. "We'll do the best we can."

"The best we can," Aunt Minty repeated with a smile. "That's just what we'll do."

She went off to the garage, where an old picnic

table of great length was stored on its side against the back wall. It broke down into pieces and wasn't as heavy as it looked, and they were able, between the three of them, to carry it out and over the grass to the garden.

Next, Aunt Minty brought out an old lace tablecloth and put it on. The picnic table was instantly transformed into an elegant party table. Nellie ran for the cups, and set them carefully in place. They were going to need chairs, that was clear.

"Do you think the flower children would mind the kitchen stools?" Aunt Minty asked. "I have some extras in the cellar, too."

"Not at all," Nellie replied. "They don't care about things like chairs." She went off to find some forks and spoons and some little plates, all of which the book's illustration showed. It also showed tremendous silver candlesticks, but:

"I don't think we need those," Nellie said to Aunt Minty. "Or those bows and ribbons that are hanging off the chairs. They would be too much trouble."

"Perhaps Mr. Bellwether did get a little carried

away with decorations. People used to in those days," Aunt Minty said. "Can we do without the little cakes as well? I'm not sure you can even buy them anymore."

"Of course!" Nellie said. "Cookies will be just as good."

Olivia found herself rather pushed aside by all this preparation. She sat on the porch pretending to read, until Aunt Minty approached and handed her the clippers.

"Would you like to cut some flowers for the vase?" she asked. "A big armful would be nice, to brighten up the table."

"Aunt Minty," Olivia said in a low voice, "this is not a good idea. Nellie is going to feel tricked and be hurt in the end."

"How do you mean?" Aunt Minty asked, far too casually and gaily.

"Well, nothing is going to happen. The countercharm won't work."

"And who says it won't?" Aunt Minty inquired sweetly.

"Well, it won't!" Olivia said. "I mean, how can it?"

"We'll just have to wait and see, won't we?" Aunt Minty replied, sounding so much like Nellie in one of her stubborn moments that Olivia glanced at her in alarm. She stood up and went to cut the flowers with a grim expression.

By lunchtime, the table was finished. The blue teapot sat ready at one end, and everything was so pretty and so almost like the book that a feeling developed in the air of something special about to happen.

Olivia looked more worried than ever at this prospect, but Nellie was in high spirits.

"The Silent Child would be so happy!" she crowed, walking up and down the flower beds. "Soon her friends will come back and the party will start, just the way it was before."

Aunt Minty smiled. "I can't wait for it either," she said. "But wait we must. There's no telling how long a countercharm will take to work. Minutes, hours, days: charms have no sense of time. The best thing we can do is go away and not stare. Shall we head for the kitchen? I'm hungry as a horse."

"I'm hungry as a mountain lion!" Nellie yelled, and grabbing Aunt Minty's hand, she yanked her through the porch door.

"Lord preserve us!" Olivia heard Aunt Minty laugh as she was being dragged away.

And so the wait for the countercharm began. All afternoon birds flew over the table in the garden, bees buzzed inquisitively around the cookie plates, and the wind blew the paper napkins up at the edges.

"No change!" Nellie came running in to report at intervals. "Not yet!" she cried, with shining eyes that hurt Olivia just to look at.

"Ah well," Aunt Minty said. "We must have patience."

"I think there is such a thing as too much patience," Olivia muttered once in a warning tone. Neither Nellie nor Aunt Minty took the least notice.

Late in the afternoon, the wind went down and the lowering sun shone rosily upon the flowers in the vase. Then the shadows of the hedges lengthened over the table, the sun slipped below the horizon, and evening's dark cape fell. When Nellie came inside for supper, she was not quite so excited as she had been. But she put up a brave front.

"Don't worry, Livy. It will happen, I know. Charms take a lot longer than people think."

This nearly broke Olivia's heart and she decided to speak to Nellie in private. But that night in bed when she started to say something, the words stuck in her mouth because Nellie looked so small and happy and excited.

Downstairs, Olivia heard Aunt Minty clumping about with unusual energy. Once she even thought she heard her talking on the phone, and she wondered if she should get up and try to listen in. By then, though, Olivia was worn out with worry, and her head felt like a heavy weight on the pillow, so she just closed her eyes and thought of other things.

The next morning when the sun rose, the table was still standing in all its splendor in the garden. A light fog had left water droplets along the handles

of the forks and spoons.
A spider had spun a web
in the loop of the teapot's
handle. A small animal had
come and gnawed on the edge
of some cookies. Nellie dried the forks and spoons
on her shirt and rearranged the cookies so the
gnawed spots wouldn't show.

"Everything must be perfect!" she said at breakfast. "Or as perfect as we can make it," she added,
glancing quickly at Aunt Minty.

"The best we can do!" Aunt Minty said merrily,
and Nellie stopped eating to laugh out loud.

So another long day of waiting began. Olivia
fumed and fidgeted and slouched in various chairs,
but Nellie went busily about thinking of more things
to do.

She helped Aunt Minty make lemonade tea. She
swept off the porch with a broom. In the afternoon,
she brought armloads of her animals downstairs and
positioned them like a theater audience on the
porch steps. She brought Ellis Bellwether's book

down too, and opened it to the right story, and left it lying on a table "so everyone can see how it really happened."

"But it hasn't happened!" Olivia couldn't help bursting out. "It hasn't and it won't. Not if you wait a hundred years! Can't you see that, Nellie? It's only a story!" She stamped off the porch and headed upstairs to read by herself.

She was hardly through the door when she heard Nellie ask Aunt Minty, "We won't have to wait a hundred years for the countercharm to work, will we?"

"A hundred years! I certainly hope not!" Aunt Minty replied. "By then our beautiful table would have fallen down and rotted."

The two of them went out into the garden to see that everything was ready. A squirrel was trying to eat the cookies again; they shooed him away. The water in the vase of cut flowers was low; they filled it.

They pulled a few weeds, though the beds looked amazingly neat. After all the digging that had gone on in recent weeks, the worst of the crabgrass and dead leaves was cleared away. The flowers showed up brighter than they had in years, which pleased Aunt Minty very much. She went about the garden speaking to them in a soft, happy voice, as if she were carrying on a private conversation.

Through an open window upstairs, Olivia watched this odd behavior disapprovingly, then returned to her book. The room was hot and perhaps she dozed off, because all of a sudden a loud babble of voices was coming up from the garden. She got up groggily and went to look.

There, at the end of the garden, she was surprised to see the stalking forms of Jack and Morry, peering into the old tulip patch. A second later, Jill came into view, wearing a brilliant red ribbon in her hair and eating a cookie.

Next was Leo, carrying one of his awful yellow trucks and followed by the nanny. There was also an unknown older girl with a butterfly net, and another girl doing cartwheels down the length of the lawn. They weren't very good cartwheels. Olivia knew she could do better. She gave a little hop of joy at the window to see, all at once, so many people in a place that had been closed up and empty for weeks and weeks. It was almost as if the Green-Skins' spell *had* been broken and the flower children had returned, and—

A terrible thought struck her.

"Nellie!" Olivia shrieked, and raced for the hall. "It's all right, Nellie. I'm coming!"

She pounded down the stairs and ran for the porch door, through which the unwelcome shapes of several grown-up visitors were visible, standing or sitting and chatting with one another. Olivia rushed onto the porch.

"Nellie! Here I am. You'll be all right. Where are you?"

There was a pause during which the people on the porch stopped talking and turned around to stare at her. Then Nellie's voice rang out like a happy chime.

"I'm right here, Livy. And look what's happened. The party's started and everybody's come!"

Eleven

It was not the party Nellie had expected, but for some reason, she didn't care. Far from it, she was pink with excitement and could not keep still. When Olivia tried to take her aside to ask if she really was "all right about this," she pulled away.

"Let me go! I'm fine. Everything's perfect!" She ran back to clear a path through her animals up the porch steps. People were tripping and stepping all over them.

Olivia did not have time to be angry at Aunt Minty right then, or even to ask how she had so sneakily arranged things, because a moment later she was swept up in the party herself. Soon she was explaining to Jack and Morry how they had found the last cup and the teapot, and showing off Ellis Bell-wether's story to an admiring crowd. Jill leaned over the book and said she could see how the cups they'd found matched the pictures, but the teapot was not the same.

"It isn't?" asked Olivia, leaning over to look too.

She saw that Jill was right. Though both were bright blue, the dug-up teapot had a blunt, square top and an angular body, while the teapot in the book had a rounder form with a tulip-shaped lid that matched the pretty cups. To Olivia, this gave final proof of the interfering hand of Aunt Minty, at least where the buried teapot was concerned.

"Don't tell Nellie," she warned Jill in a low voice. "Nellie wants to believe, so we'll just let her."

Jack and Morry, who had overheard, hooted with laughter over this. "We thought so!" Jack cried. "We knew that tea set was planted."

"Did your aunt bury the cups too, or was it some-body else?" Morry asked.

"That is still unknown," Olivia said, lifting her eyebrows so mysteriously—so exactly like Aunt

Minty, in fact—that everyone roared with laughter.

This was great fun, and a tremendous relief after going so long without friends. Not until the party actually sat down at the table, however, did Olivia understand the really important thing that was happening in the garden that afternoon. By then, she'd had time to watch Nellie more closely.

She watched her walk up to Jill and tell her to quit stealing cookies from the plates on the table, or else!

She saw her stop and listen to Leo talk about trucks for about ten seconds, and then rudely walk off.

She observed Nellie following the unknown older girl with the butterfly net and trying to get her attention by standing on her head.

She saw how angry Nellie became when the unknown older girl ignored her, and how Nellie stormed off to complain to Aunt Minty.

She saw Nellie steal a cookie herself.

Olivia saw, in other words, that everything wasn't perfect at all. Nellie still had a long way to go to join the civilized world, as Pop would have said. But she was doing all right for someone her age, especially because suddenly she didn't need to have Olivia all to herself anymore.

"Hi Livy!" Nellie called across the table as they took their seats on the stools. "Are you having a good time?"

Olivia nodded and waved back.

"Don't worry about the flower children," Nellie called. "They'll come pretty soon."

"They will?" Olivia yelled back.

"Yes! Not today, though. It's too noisy. They would feel shy about coming out."

"When will they come?"

"How should I know?" Nellie bellowed in an irritated voice. "No one ever knows about counter-charms."

Nellie was distracted then by someone sitting down next to her. It turned out to be the girl who was doing all the cartwheels. Although she couldn't do them very well yet, she was taking gymnastics lessons in the church basement and knew a lot of tips on how to get better. Soon she and Nellie were practicing hard on the grass.

"I'm not giving up!" Olivia heard Nellie shriek. "I can do it, I know. Get out of my way!"

It was at this point, as Olivia was gazing protectively at Nellie, and wondering if this new friend was a good enough person for her, that another spell seemed to get broken. Olivia felt the tiredness that had been dragging her down for weeks rise out of her bones, and a new lightness come into her. It was as if she had been planted in one place for months, and now was set free to go wherever she wanted.

And shortly, this proved to be the case, because practically the next minute, Jill was inviting her to come over to her house, and Olivia was accepting.

"Without Nellie?" Jill whispered.

"How about tomorrow?" Olivia replied.

⬩ ⬩ ⬩

While spells of an ordinary, human sort were meeting their end in the horseshoe-shaped garden that afternoon, the real, magical kind continued unbroken and seemingly unbreakable. The lost flower children did not appear that day, or the next, or the next week or the week after that.

Olivia did not find this very surprising, but Nellie's faith never wavered. She insisted on keeping the beautiful table set and ready. After the party, Aunt Minty washed the blue cups and the blue teapot and Nellie put them right back out on the lace tablecloth. She put out new paper napkins every few days, whenever the old ones got wet or blown away by the wind. She cut fresh flowers and changed the water in the vase. She kept the cookie plates filled, a never-ending job since the cookies kept disappearing at a faster and faster rate.

"Those squirrels are certainly getting after our cookies," Aunt Minty said one day, with a sharp glance at Nellie. "They don't just nibble now, they take the whole thing."

"Well, they're hungry," Nellie said. "Winter's coming, you know."

Olivia almost laughed out loud hearing this, but Aunt Minty merely said, "Hmm–mmm. Speaking of winter, I was thinking we might want to take the flower children's table down for the season. It's my experience that countercharms never work in cold weather."

Nellie was amazingly agreeable to this. Next spring would be plenty of time to try again, she said. The flowers in the garden had mostly withered anyway, and she had a lot of work to do practicing cartwheels and headstands all the time. She was taking gymnastics lessons in the church basement. Aunt Minty drove her over twice a week.

If winter wasn't quite in sight yet, fall was. The hot weather passed, the evenings grew cool. August swung around the corner into September. Pop was late. On the phone, he promised to come get them one weekend, then called back and said he was sorry, he couldn't yet. There'd been a change in his job. He had to learn a new sales route, take another trip. Give him a few more weeks and he'd have things straight.

Olivia heard the real story by listening in when he talked to Aunt Minty.

"They laid me off, Mint. Can you believe it? A time like this and they drop me in the gutter. Don't tell the girls—they'd just be upset. Can you put Olivia in a school there? I'll need another month or two to get on my feet. . . . You're a saint, Mint. What would I do without you?"

Not so long ago, this conversation would have made Olivia feel dumped at Aunt Minty's all over again. She would have had to stay awake all night worrying about what would happen and trying to figure out some way to tell Nellie that wouldn't make her cry.

Now, Olivia was glad they were staying. Secretly, she hoped they could stay the whole fall. Nellie wouldn't mind; even she could tell that Pop wasn't sounding very organized on the phone. Meanwhile, life at Aunt Minty's had started to settle down.

Aunt Minty herself still needed help, of course. There were a hundred of Nellie's pitfalls still lurking at her feet, and the threat, in bad moments, of new golden rules. You never knew when Aunt Minty would overstep and decide to take matters into her own hands. Olivia was working on her, though, and getting to trust her a little more, and someday, who knew?—she might turn out to be quite reliable.

"Is Jill in the school I'll be going to?" Olivia asked her that night when they sat down to dinner, completely forgetting that she'd heard this listening in on the phone. She put her hand over her mouth and waited with thumping heart.

Aunt Minty showed no signs of noticing, however. She never even glanced up from under her ratty straw hat, which she'd neglected to take off that evening, as usual.

"Girls," she said. "I'm sick and tired of everybody protecting everybody from hearing things in this family. I think you have a right to know and I'm going to tell you. Your father's lost his job. You'll be staying on here with me this fall until he finds another one. If I were you, Olivia, I'd call up Jill right after dinner and ask her what school she goes to. We'll go around tomorrow and get you in."

These were such wide-open, honest words to Olivia's sneaking, undercover ears that she couldn't, for a moment, think of what to say back. She just stared at Aunt Minty's hat, with all its holes and the yellowy-white hair sprouting through, and thought how it didn't look that bad after all.

Twelve

For many weeks after the party table was taken down—and its lace cloth folded away in a bottom drawer, and the blue tea set stored in the dining room cupboard—the old horseshoe-shaped garden was left alone and hardly visited at all.

From her upstairs window, Olivia saw the flower shrubs turn soft yellows and browns and begin to bed down for winter. The birds departed for points south. Squirrels and mice whose home nests had been in the stone wall now moved to more protected quarters underground, and there was a general battening down of hatches and stockpiling of nuts and seeds.

The weather was turning increasingly raw and cold when, toward the end of October, a day arrived that was as warm and blue as any summer day. It happened to be a Saturday when no one had made plans to do anything or go anywhere, and so, one by one, first Nellie, and then Aunt Minty, and finally Olivia wandered out to the garden porch to find the sun.

The porch was a place no one had been for some time. They were all too busy now. Olivia went off early on the bus to Jill's school, which was now her school too. Afterward, she was often invited back to Jill's house or to the homes of other friends. She was meeting a lot of people. Many more students were in her classes than at her old school, which meant dozens of new faces and names to learn.

There was also a complicated pattern of stairs and floors and rooms and corners to get used to, since the school itself was so enormous. Olivia was forever losing her way in the halls, or coming up against a locked door. One morning, she climbed up too many flights of stairs and ended up on the roof, where she was immediately trapped because the door swung shut behind her and locked.

"What did you do?" Jill asked, in horror, at lunch.

"Oh, I just yelled and waved my sweater around until someone on the playground saw me," Olivia said. "No one could find the roof door for a while. The principal said I must be the only person besides the janitor who ever figured out how to get up there."

"You spoke to the principal?" Jill said, looking even more shocked.

"Not really," Olivia said, modestly. "He spoke to me."

She was not always so confident and brave. On many dark nights, she missed Mama terribly. She still filled in the map of heaven when she was lonely or scared, and kept the sad place in her head sealed up and hidden away from outside eyes. Aunt Minty knew it was there, though she never asked about it. Sometimes in the evening, after Nellie was asleep, Olivia would go downstairs and they would talk about things. By and large, though, she was all right most of the time, and she felt that, slowly but certainly, she was getting to know her way around.

"Like you, Mama," Olivia would occasionally whisper toward the ceiling late at night. "We are doing it together," she would add, for it seemed to her that somewhere amidst the mountains and oceans of heaven, her mother was listening, and smiling down at her, and getting used to things too.

Nellie had been very busy also, progressing from gymnastics in the church basement to a kindergarten upstairs, which ran five days a week from nine A.M. to one P.M.

This seemed to Nellie like a long time away by herself, and she, unlike Olivia, was never embarrassed to see Aunt Minty arrive to pick her up. No matter how small and wrinkly Aunt Minty looked, or how much hair was sprouting out the holes in her hat, Nellie always screeched, "Aunt Minty!" the moment she saw her. Then she would hurl herself across the floor into the old woman's arms.

"If you don't come get us pretty soon, Nellie won't want to leave," Olivia warned Pop one day on the phone. "She told me her animals are the happiest they've ever been."

"Well, tell her to hold on," Pop answered. "I've almost got this new job. Except there's a chance we might have to move to Canada."

"Canada!" Olivia cried. "That's the worst idea I ever heard of!"

She and Pop had begun to tell all kinds of things like this to each other on the telephone. At Aunt Minty's suggestion, Pop never asked for private chats anymore, which made Olivia feel much happier.

"I am a person who likes to know what is happening," she explained to him.

"And who'll find out anyway," Nellie added, "so you might as well tell her."

Now, on this warm October Saturday, the sisters settled together on the steps of the sunny porch while Aunt Minty stood behind them, gazing fondly out at her flower beds. She sniffed the air and declared it a jewel of a day, in fact the very day she'd been waiting for.

"For what?" Nellie asked.

"For planting daffodils," Aunt Minty replied. "You two girls did such a job clearing the garden this summer that it's raised my spirits. I believe I can make something of this place again."

"You mean bring the garden back to how it used to be?" Olivia asked.

"I do," said Aunt Minty. "It'll take some serious cleaning out next April, and I'll hire a worker for that when the time comes. But we can start right now by putting in some daffodil bulbs. They need to set over the winter if they're to make a spring appearance."

"Well, where are these bulbs?" Nellie demanded.

Aunt Minty went back in the house and brought forth a paper bag of brown, onion-shaped bulbs (Nellie had expected the glass ones used in lamps), and another bag of chalky bonemeal to sprinkle in the soil. Nellie and Olivia fetched two trowels and a shovel from the garage. A short while later, all three were at work digging holes on either side of the stone bench, which was the perfect place for creamy-white Mount Hood daffodils, Aunt Minty said, because they'd look beautiful with the red tulips and the bluebells when they all came up together next spring.

"Were you really a famous gardener?" Olivia asked, pushing her shovel into the earth with one foot. "You know so much about growing plants and flowers."

"Famous?" said Aunt Minty. "I wouldn't say so. I've spent my whole life digging in this one garden. Whatever I know, I've learned from it. There's no harder teacher than a garden, I'd say."

"That's how the Silent Child learned," said Nellie, who still kept Ellis Bellwether's book in her bed.

"Did she?" murmured Aunt Minty. She had stopped listening and was intent on placing the daffodil bulbs in their holes and working bonemeal into the soil around them.

"The Silent Child had only one garden in her whole life too," Nellie went on. She stopped digging and looked up. "And she talked to the flowers as if they were friends. And she was the most helpful—" Here Olivia stopped digging too, and stared at Aunt Minty, who continued to work, unaware of the sisters' eyes and, seemingly, of Nellie's words as well, so engrossed was she in her planting.

"Aunt Minty? Were you the smallest child?" Olivia asked suddenly, in a loud voice.

"Was I . . . ?" Aunt Minty glanced up. "Well, I don't know. Why do you ask that? I was the youngest in my family, if that's what you mean."

Olivia and Nellie exchanged amazed and startled glances. They hardly knew how to begin to ask the next question. Nellie waited for Olivia to ask because she was older and knew better words to use at such a delicate moment, and Olivia waited for Nellie because she was younger and could speak more boldly. There was a long pause during which Aunt Minty went on digging without looking up, and the garden seemed to pass into one of its absolutely still, magical trances. Then came a grating sound.

"Glory!" said Aunt Minty. "I've struck something here."